TISSUE, PLEASE!

by

Lisa Kopelke

SIMON AND SCHUSTER
LONDON NEW YORK SYDNEY

SIMON AND SCHUSTER

First published in Great Britain in 2004 by Simon & Schuster UK Ltd
Africa House, 64-78 Kingsway, London WC2B 6AH

Originally published in 2004 by Simon and Schuster Books for Young Readers,
an imprint of Simon & Schuster Children's Publishing Division, New York

Text and illustrations copyright © 2004 Lisa Kopelke

The right of Lisa Kopelke to be identified as the author and illustrator of this work has been
asserted by her in accordance with the Copyright, Designs and Patents Act, 1988

Book designed by Greg Stadnyk
The text for this book is set in Green and Neo Neo
The illustrations are rendered in acrylic

A CIP catalogue record for this book is available from the British Library upon request

ISBN 0-743-49004-5
Manufactured in China
1 3 5 7 9 10 8 6 4 2

To Claire

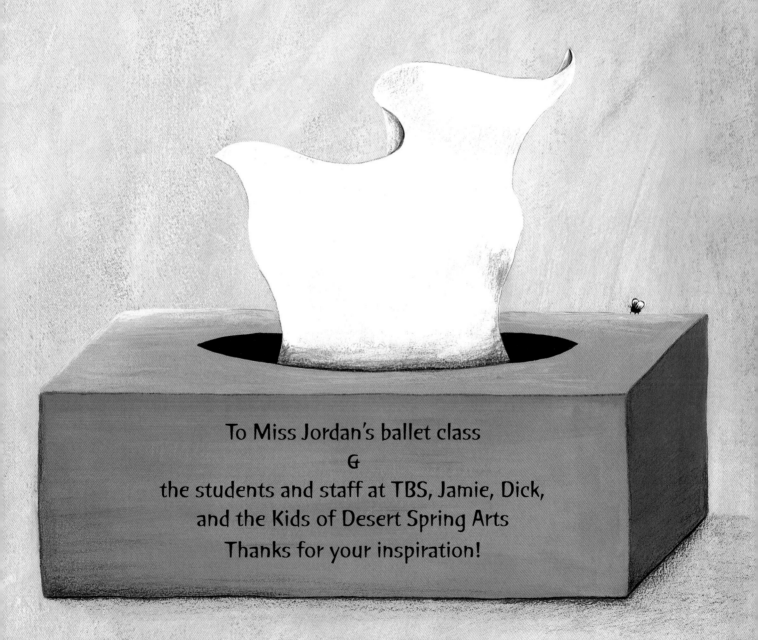

To Miss Jordan's ballet class
&
the students and staff at TBS, Jamie, Dick,
and the Kids of Desert Spring Arts
Thanks for your inspiration!

Frog and his friends did *everything* together.

At breaktime they played hopscotch
and skipped together.

In the classroom they sat at the same table and worked together. And when they had runny noses, they sniffled and snuffled together.

"Snerrrfle!" they announced as they wiped their noses on their arms.
"Ahem!" Mr Sage replied.

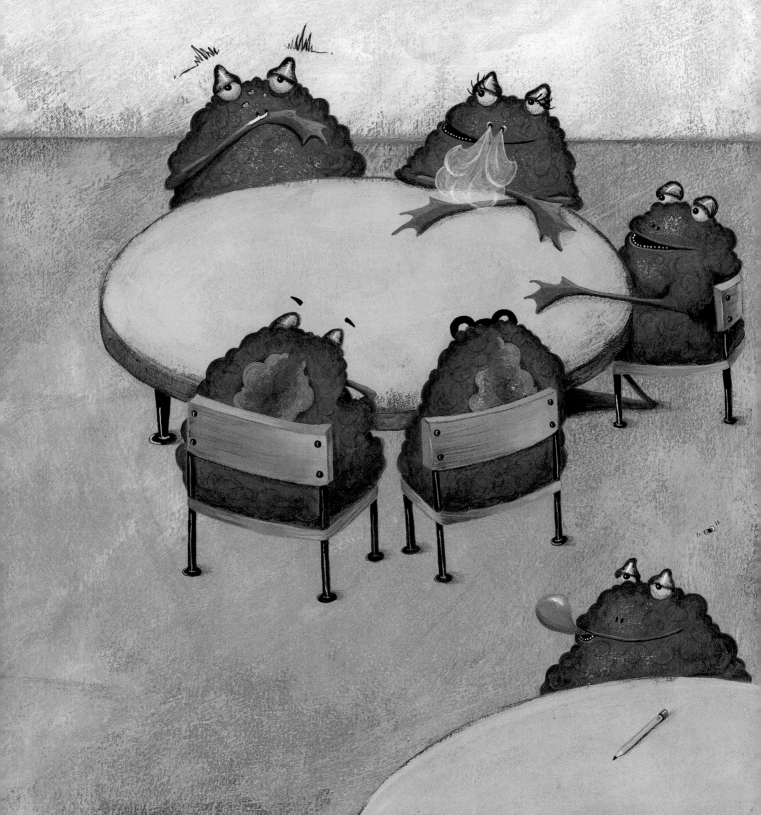

After school Frog and his friends rode
their bikes to dance class together.
They were practising for their show.

Frog loved his ballet class.

Lately he was finding it hard to concentrate. He still had a runny nose, which made it difficult to dance.

"schnorrrkle!" Frog rang out.

When his friends heard him, they remembered their noses were runny too. Soon the whole class was one huge chorus of sniffles and snuffles as they wiped their noses on their arms.

Miss Tutu was so disgusted, all she could say was
"Yuck!"

At home Frog was enjoying his dinner– potato-bug soup with fish crackers. He was in the middle of a big slurp when he realised he needed to sniffle.

"Snerrrf – " Frog started.

"That's not polite at the dinner table," interrupted his father.

Frog's mother leaped out of the room and came back with a box of tissues.

"Please, use this instead,"
she suggested.

Frog blew his nose into the tissue and was amazed
at how well it worked. His nose felt great!

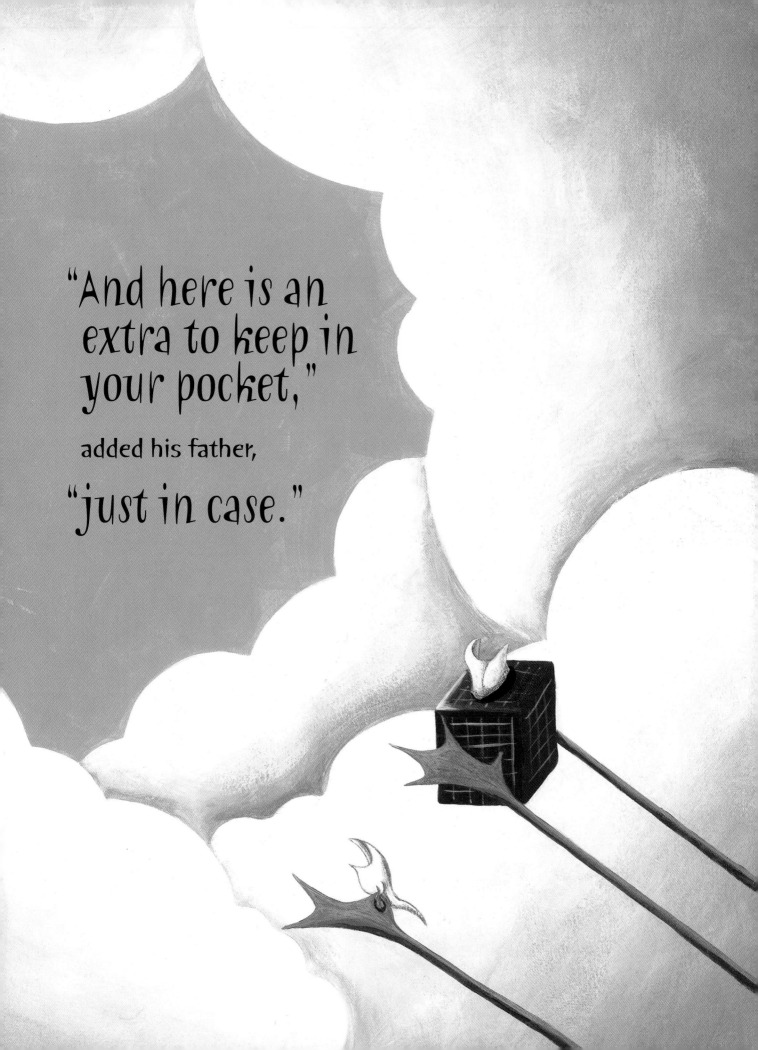

"And here is an extra to keep in your pocket,"

added his father,

"just in case."

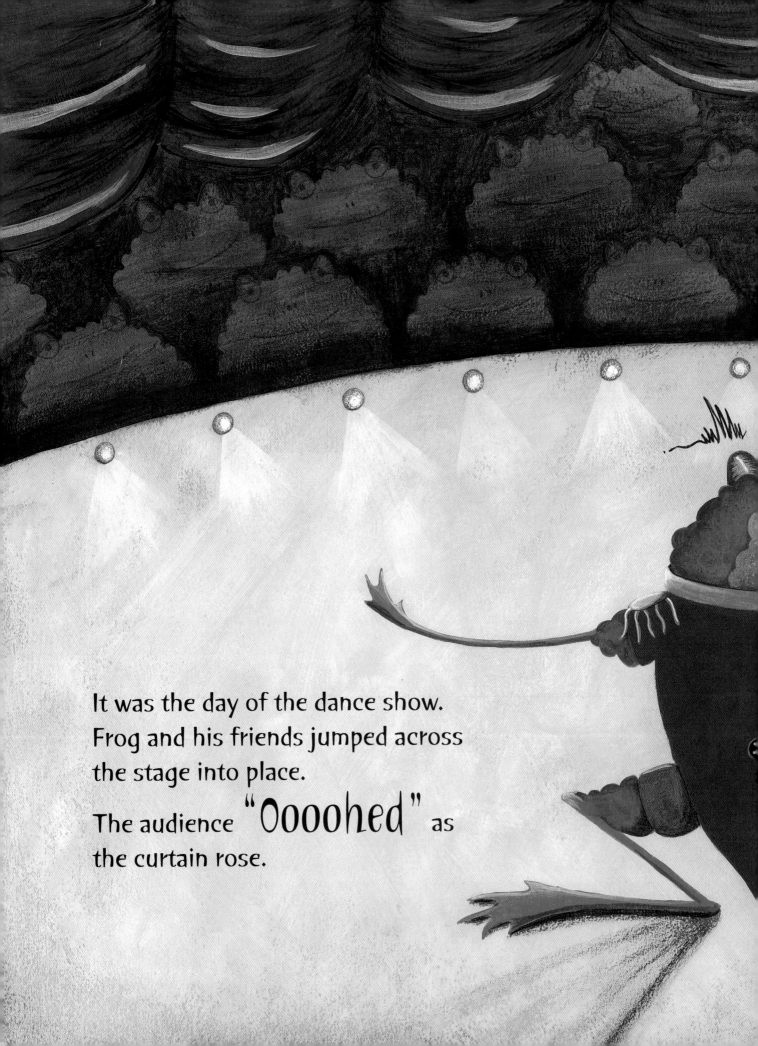

It was the day of the dance show.
Frog and his friends jumped across
the stage into place.

The audience "Oooohed" as
the curtain rose.

In the middle of his grand plié, Frog's
nose began to run again. So he sniffled.
It wasn't working.

Frog was getting ready for a gigantic snuffle, when he noticed his teacher watching him offstage.

Frog suddenly remembered . . . a tissue!

Frog quickly hopped over and took
a tissue out of the box on the
piano and hopped back into place.
He blew his nose and finished his
plié in one graceful move, waving
the tissue high above his head.

Frog's friends were inspired.

They each pirouetted across the stage,
grabbing a tissue mid-twirl.

"Mmmmmmmpfff,"
they blew in a loud symphony.

Then one by one they waved their tissues over their heads, danced over and flung them into the bin.

Miss Tutu was so proud, all she could say was "Bravo!"

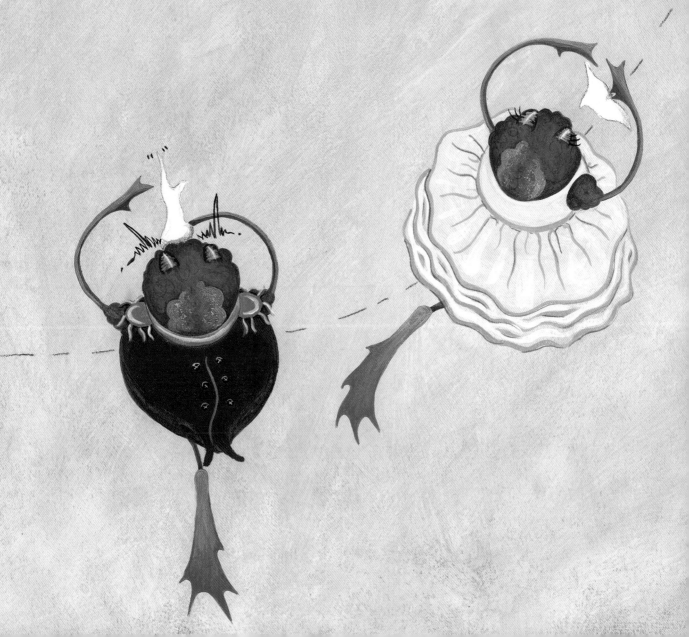

The audience was impressed.
"Encore!" they yelled.

And from that day on the *Dance of the Tissue-Box Fairies* was the grand finale of every show.